Tad Tr

by Liza Charlesworth

ISBN: 978-1-338-78273-8
Illustrated by Kevin Zimmer
Copyright © 2021 by Liza Charlesworth. All rights reserved.
Published by Scholastic Inc., 557 Broadway, New York, NY 10012

10 9 8 7 6 5 4 3 2 1   68   21 22 23 24 25 26 27/0

Printed in Jiaxing, China. First printing, June 2021.

■SCHOLASTIC

Tad Troll did **not** like to swing.
It made him mad.

GRRR!

Tad Troll did **not** like to skate.
It made him mad.

GRRR!

Tad Troll did **not** like to shop.
It made him mad.

Tad Troll did **not** like to climb.
It made him mad.

GRRR!

Tad Troll did **not** like to dance.
It made him mad.

Tad Troll DID like to draw.
It made him glad!